aLL of YOU was SINGING

To those who have heard in sounds,
the music we listen for;
To those who have given us music,
so we too can sing

— *R.L.*

To Silence,
which serves to temper the sound

— *E..Y.*

To the Aztecs in Mexico and their neighbors to the South, the Mayans, the world is suffused with an almost supernatural quality of aliveness. Colors, flowers, wind, water—even the silence between the stars—are seen as symbols of the workings of the universe and of our place within it. The Aztecs believed in a complex system of gods, who personified many of the forces of nature. The sun itself was a god who lived in a house in the sky where there was much singing and dancing. Another god, Tezcatlipoca, like many Aztec gods, took on different forms, but most often represented night. It was Tezcatlipoca who asked Quetzalcoatl—an important Aztec god who represented the spirit and the wind—to journey to the sun and bring the musicians there back to Earth.

ALL OF YOU WAS SINGING is a retelling of this myth about how music came to Earth. As with all myths, many meanings can be read into it. My own sense of this myth is the profound importance of music to the well-being of life. To sing is an affirmation of the melody and rhythm of life. And such singing continues, as in this Aztec song, even after us:

My flowers shall not perish
Nor shall my chants cease
They spread, they scatter.

–R.L.

aLL of YOU was SINGING

RICHARD LEWIS

art by ED YOUNG

ATHENEUM   1991   NEW YORK

Collier Macmillan Canada
TORONTO

Maxwell Macmillan International Publishing Group
NEW YORK   OXFORD   SINGAPORE   SYDNEY

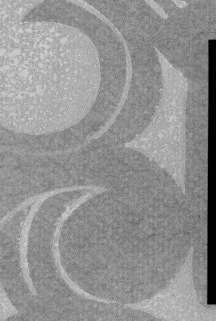

When things were beginning,
there was water
everywhere.

*And the earth-monster
swam everywhere,*

*eating everything
it saw.*

From out of everywhere,
there came two serpents
who tore
the earth-monster
in half.

The bottom of the monster
rose to become the heavens.
And the top of the monster
fell to become the earth.

And before there was night or day
on the earth and in the sky,
there was a terrible darkness. . . .

And the sky, speaking to the earth, said:
I am your sky.
You are my earth.

From your eyes, the gods made springs
of cold water.
From your mouth, they made the deep caves
and echoing caverns.

From your skin, they brought the lawns
of jeweled flowers.
From your hair, they fashioned the long grass
and the noble trees.

And the first sound I heard in my heavens
was the sound
of moving air
becoming
the wind.

The sound of the wind grew
and became the glowing of stars.

The sound of the wind grew
and became the music of the sun.

But whenever I, the sky, reached toward you,
the earth,
the music of the sun stood still,
and you, the earth, which had light to see
the colors of your flowers and birds…
you had no music;
you wore upon your body only
a mist of silence.

My sadness shook, pleading with the wind:

"Wind, we must bring music to the earth.
We must bring music to the waking dawn.
We must bring music to the dreaming man.
We must bring music to the moving waters and
the flying birds.
Wind, life upon the earth must be music.

"Wind, go to the house of the sun, where you shall
find a music whose burning sounds bring me
my light.

"Wind, bring back to the silent earth these
flowers of sounds;
bring back clusters of the most
beautiful music."

And the wind, hearing my plea,
gathered into itself
all of your earth's silence
and, in a great rush of air,
swept past the roofs of my sky,
where it found the sun
and the melodies of its music,
playing in a nest of light.

In the east, the singer in white sang
the songs of the newborn.

In the west, the singer in red played
the songs of love and war.

In the north, the singer in blue sang
the songs of wandering clouds.

In the south, the singer in yellow sang
the songs of gold.

All of my sky was filled with the surging
of wind,
And the sun cried to the musicians:

"The earth's wind comes closer.
Do not answer the wind."

And the wind cried:

"Come, come, musicians of the sun.
The earth is calling you."

Their arguing made my hands become
claws of lightning,
and my voice become the fury of thunder,
and in the blackness of my clouds,
the sun drowned.

Afraid, the musicians of the sun
ran into the arms of the wind,
which gently carried their melodies
into the arms
of you,
the earth.

Your silence opened.

Your waking dawn sang.

Your dreaming man sang.

Your moving waters and your flying
birds sang.

Your waiting mother sang.

All of you was singing.

Music had come to the earth.

ALL OF YOU WAS SINGING is a rendering of an Aztec myth recorded in MEXICAN AND CENTRAL AMERICAN MYTHOLOGY, by Irene Nicholson, published by Hamlyn in 1967. Except for the very beginning of my rendering, which is based on Ms. Nicholson's discussion of a Nahua creation myth, the body of my adaptation is centered on a translation of a sixteenth-century Nahua manuscript by Ms. Nicholson.
—*R.L.*

Text copyright © 1991 by Richard Lewis
Illustrations copyright © 1991 by Ed Young

Atheneum
Macmillan Publishing Company
866 Third Avenue
New York, NY 10022

Collier Macmillan Canada, Inc.
1200 Eglinton Avenue East
Suite 200
Don Mills, Ontario M3C 3N1

First edition
Printed in Hong Kong by South China Printing Company (1988) Ltd.
1 2 3 4 5 6 7 8 9 10

Library of Congress Cataloging-in-Publication Data
Lewis, Richard.
All of you was singing/by Richard Lewis; illustrated by Ed
Young.—1st ed.
p.   cm.
Summary: A lyrical account of the earth's creation and the advent
of music.
ISBN 0-689-31596-1
[1. Creation—Fiction. 2. Music—Fiction.] I. Young, Ed, ill.
II. Title.
PZ7.L5877A1   1991
[E]—dc20   89-18263   CIP   AC